F L
&
PLEASURE

A Novella

Ash Ericmore

Written by: Ash Ericmore

Copyright © 2021 Ash Ericmore

All Rights Reserved. This is a work of fiction. No part of this publication may be reproduced, distributed, or transmitted in any form or by any means, except in the case of brief quotations embodied in critical reviews.

ISBN: 9798801424736

CHAPTER 1

Owen kept his fingers wrapped tightly around her throat. He wrung them gently, massaging the life from her slow. Real slow. He didn't want to go too far. Not yet. *Not yet.* She was laying on the floor, him hunched over her. Squeezing. Making sure to not snap the neck. Just stop the flow of air. She was staring up at him. Her eyes bulging, slightly. Her pretty blond hair was dishevelled.

She looked surprised.

Her fingers were wrapped around his wrists. She was trying to stop him. *Trying.* She wasn't trying hard enough. The strength was gone from her grip. He had a couple of scratch marks on his skin, but nothing that wouldn't heal in a couple of days with some antiseptic. She'd stopped kicking. Probably meant that the blood in her legs didn't have any oxygen in them anymore.

Probably.

Who knows? Last time he did this, the bitch just croaked on him. He went too far. Pushed her body too hard. Owen smiled at the thought, squeezing harder. He caught himself. Dropped the smile. Stopping. No. He didn't want this one to die like this. Not this time. She should live. For now. The smile returned. She let go of his wrists, her fingers slipping from his flesh. Flopping lifelessly to the floor.

He let go of her neck. It was hard to release her. The adrenaline made him hold on like she was a steering wheel and he was hurtling towards an eighteen wheeler on the wrong side of the motorway.

His fingers ached from the effort. The intensity.

She slumped loose to the floor.

Owen realised he was shaking. Just slightly. Like he'd just gotten off a roller coaster. Like that one on the beach when he was a kid. Looked so fucking scary. In retrospect, it was probably as unsafe as fuck, but those were the days. His eyes went from his hands, still out, palm up, in front of him, to the woman on the floor. She was still breathing. Well, breathing again. He could see her breasts rise and fall. She was half undressed. Topless. Still had on her miniskirt. Fishnets. High heels. Owen wiped his palms down on his jeans like he was dirty. Sticky. From touching her. He was breathing hard, himself. Probably needed some more cardio. Rolled his shoulders. Aches from the effort burning across his back. Neck. Man, he needed to get down the gym.

He went over to the window and glanced out around the side of the curtains. Into the night. Made sure there was no one outside the house. Watching. Bitch had made noise. Too much noise.

And this was a nice neighbourhood. Cul-de-sac. Very desirable, according to Zoopla, anyway. All the houses were new build. Made like shit, obviously. The windows were too small. The insides too dark. But they were detached. Had driveways and garages. Small kitchens, he mused. Would have liked a bigger kitchen. Stock, square back gardens.

He'd tried digging into the grass once, and had found that after about a foot of soil he hit chalk. No way he was ever going to plant much out there. Still. Got a little shed now. About eight foot square. Big enough for a workbench and a lawn mower.

Oh. There was no one in the street, by the way. Owen let the curtain drop back to hang and turned back to the woman on the rug in front of the sofa. She was still out. He went over to the small cupboard under the stairs. Yes. It was one of *those* new builds with the front door straight into the open-plan living room, diner, with the kitchen off the back. Stairs in the middle of the living room. Not enough room to swing a cat. But at least he had a cupboard in the lounge.

He held the door open.

Somewhere to keep the stuff he needed.

He pulled the holdall out and went back to the sofa, slumping down on the cushions next to the woman on the floor. Barely a woman. More a girl. Probably would have gotten asked for ID if she'd been looking to hook up in a decent place. But she hadn't. Ratty fucking club. Full of old perverts and teenage girls. He looked down on her body. She was going to wake up soon. Best get on with it.

Owen opened the bag and pulled out a ball-gag. He'd brought it online at a sex shop. Saved the embarrassment of going somewhere and buying something like that over the counter. There would be human interaction. He didn't want to be judged. They would know why he wanted it. Well, they thought they did. And they'd judge him. He could have made something, but why re-invent the wheel? These things were designed to keep a bitch quiet, and be impossible to remove. And it only cost a few quid. He'd put a not-inconsiderable amount of items in his basket while he was on the sex site, but had removed most of them before going to the checkout. No point in having them, he supposed.

He looked down at himself. It briefly crossed his mind that he shouldn't be doing this, then he forgot that, as his eyes settled on her. On the floor. He reached down. Pushed the ball into her mouth and yanked the leather straps around her head. He tightened them at the back, getting the buckle all caught up in her hair. Fuck it. Didn't matter.

CHAPTER 2

Tied spread eagle to the bed. Ball-gag in. Naked now. Owen looked down at her. She'd woken up as he was sitting in the armchair at the end of the bed, in the corner of the room. He was reading one of those flyers you get through the door from the local takeaways. New one. Usually was. For some reason they changed hands pretty quick in the area. On Just Eat they had nearly a hundred of the fucking things locally, and yeah, sure, he liked to look at all the new places but he pretty much stuck to the tried and tested. One kebab shop. One pizza place. No fish and chips. Battered fish didn't travel well. Got all greasy. He looked from the menu to her. She was staring at him. She hadn't made a sound. Not that it mattered. Not with the gag in.

Back to the menu.

Chinese.

Never was much of a fan of Chinese food. Not from a takeaway, anyway. And the place looked expensive.

He stood. Put the menu on the nightstand next to the lamp, alarm clock, and shitty fantasy book he'd picked up from the charity shop because he liked the cover. Book was awful, though.

She was watching him. Silent. Waiting. Good girl. Well behaved. Trained by her father, perhaps. Owen let his eyes ride down her skin. She had pert, young breasts. Fine, smooth, skin. Her eyes were bright and clear, even though she was crying. Just a little. Made the mascara run down her face. Probably

the cheap stuff. She didn't look old enough to have
the money to buy anything other than shit from the
pound shop. Something like that, anyway. Owen
pulled his t-shirt over his head. Tossed it to the floor.
He could see her eyes dart around his body. Looking
down at himself, just lately, his chest hair had started
to go grey. *Comes with age*, he guessed. As did a lot
of other things.

Came and went.

Owen smiled down at the girl. Long forgotten her
name, even if she'd given it. Might have—probably
was—fake anyway. Didn't matter now. Now she was
Zoe. He smiled at Zoe. She didn't smile back.
Couldn't, really. But that was okay. He unhooked his
belt. Let it hang loose. Undid the button at the waist
of his jeans. Then unzipped them. Let them sort of
hang open. Thought it looked cool. Sexy.

He looked down at her body. She was quivering.
Excited.

Owen pushed the toe of his boot into the heel of
the other and pushed it off. Kicked it away to the side
of the bed. Did the same with his socked toes to the
other. Then he sat, next to Zoe, and pulled his socks
off. He'd thought about it. There was no sexy way to
pull socks off. So be it. She was going to see him
unsexily pull them off. Didn't matter. He glanced to
her as he tossed the second sock to the floor, close to
his boots. They were slightly moist. Sweat from the
club. Then the effort. But she didn't know that.

He stood again. Pulled his jeans off. They weren't
tight or anything. He was far too old for that. They
just dropped down to this ankles. He stepped out of
them. Then did the same with his boxers. He was

wearing clean ones. He'd ordered some tight things that were supposed to show off your size but they hadn't come yet. Fucking *Wish*. So he'd settled with clean boxers. Black ones.

He stood over her. As naked as she was, now. She squirmed more now he was naked. Probably the excitement. Probably. She was pulling on the handcuffs that he had used to restrain her to the bed. One pair on each wrist and different ones on her ankles. He'd found that, at the same online sex shop as the one the ball-gag came from, you could buy bespoke foot restraints. Hand cuffs for feet. Foot cuffs, he supposed. So they, the hand cuffs and the ball gag were what stayed in his basket.

Owen bent forward and rested his hand on the girl's belly. It was jiggling slightly. She was only a thin little thing, but her belly jiggled. As soon as his flesh met hers, she stopped. Stopped moving altogether. Like she froze.

He smiled as warmly as he could at her. "Do you want me, Zoe?" he asked. His voice was quiet. Deep. Warm. Like it was the last time he was with Zoe.

Zoe shook her head. Hard. Violently. She didn't want to be with him.

Owen removed his hand. Looking at her. Looking in her eyes. He was sad that she didn't. But then he looked down at his body. It was shrivelling with age. Hanging in places it shouldn't. Grey hairs where there should have been darker ones.

He stood.

"But I still want you," he said, staring off into the room, looking at nothing in particular. "After all these years, I still do." He turned, and looked at her. She was still crying. Harder now. Black smears down her face, disappearing into her hair. But she'd stopped struggling. His eyes fell on her cunt. Badly shaved like a teenager who couldn't quite grow a beard. He bent down and ran the ends of his fingers over her baldish mound. "I still do."

CHAPTER 3

Owen looked down at her. He could smell her, even from where he was standing. Something cheap. She was sweating now. It wasn't that hot in the house, although he had turned the heating up—rather thoughtfully—before he had gone out for the evening. She was young and beautiful.

Yes.

Owen straddled across her. He put one knee each side of her thighs, and sat back, on her knees, giving him the best possible view of her naked body. And her, his. He slowly ran the tips of his fingers over her skin. Goose bumps rising and falling as their flesh touched. He looked deep into her eyes. Fear.

And he could feel the anger inside him. It was rising. It was in his gut, then. It was like he'd eaten too much fruit and he was going to shit soon. But it was moving. And not in that direction. The twist of the stomach was next. He could feel it just starting to take grip. Pushed his hands down flat from the fingertips to the palms. She was clammy under his touch. Owen leaned forward and smelt her. Sweat, mixed with cheap perfume. Made her smell like a whore. Like a cheap whore who'd just fucked some john. He sat back upright and raised his hand, slapping it down onto her belly. Open palmed. The loud *shpap* filled the room, before it was gone. She screamed, hidden behind the ball-gag. Good. It was doing a wonderful job of silencing the cow. He lifted his hand. A large red imprint stayed behind. Burnt onto her skin. Inflamed. He grinned into her face.

Finally, some satisfaction. She had her eyes closed now. Probably concentrating on the pain.

The redness.

Owen clawed his hands, fingers rigid, and curved, and then drew then hard down her body, starting with the chest. Over her breasts, tearing at her nipples. Onto her belly. Streaks of white and yellow appeared as the blood was forced from the surface, and then flooded with red. He sat back. Eight stripes on the whore's body. She was crying and screaming. Her head held to the side so that she couldn't look at him.

Like that might protect her.

Blood was coming from one of her areolas. Maybe he needed to cut his nails. He looked at them. Not long. Clean, too. He smiled to himself as she wouldn't look at him. Then he slapped her hard on the tits. They bounced a little. Too small for that sort of play. Shuffled back down her body a little. Jabbed the two longest fingers on his right hand in her cunt. She twisted as she screamed. It was louder. Without the gag, would have screamed the house down no doubt. Owen liked that. He liked a screamer, but the other houses in the street might not. Not on a work night. School night for some of them. The Wilson's had an eight year old. She probably wouldn't want to hear the screaming. The Tennent's had a fourteen year old boy. He might knock one out to the sound of it. Owen looked at Zoe. Yes. She would probably sate the needs of a fourteen year old. Fuck him proper. He withdrew his fingers. Sniffed them. Touched his tongue to the tip of his middle finger. She didn't taste like much. He wrinkled his nose.

So be it.

Owen got from the bed and padded naked to the chest of drawers in the corner. Opened the middle one. Never keep anything you want found in the top or bottom drawer of a chest. That was the first place people looked.

He glanced across to the girl. "I want to fuck you now." He looked down at himself and shook his head almost unperceivably. He pulled a blade from the drawer. A simple long handled one. Walked it over to the bed. "Hm," he grunted, waving the blade in front of her eyes. She thrashed more.

Then he cut her.

Slid the blade into her body above the pubic mound and started to cut away the meat. The girl screamed in agony as he dug around, blood sloshing from her body. He created a cave, a deep well, poking with the end of the knife looking for something. Something specific. When he found it, he made a triumphant sound. Something guttural. He carved a few cuts and then pushed his hand in.

Retrieving his prize.

Pulling the girl's uterus out, a clammy, sticky mess. He looked up to her face. Grinning. She wasn't moving. Possibly still alive, and just unconscious from the shock. He looked down at the wound, geysering blood out onto his sheets. But not for long. "I have it," he said to her. "Look, Zoe. I have it."

He brought the lump of clotting flesh to his lips and kissed it.

CHAPTER 4

Nobody would miss the girl for days. Owen dragged the corpse from the bed onto a tarp he'd brought at B and Q. Wrapped it up. Held it with bungies. The morning after would be easier for some people. They just had to flap their hands and make the whore leave. He had to take them somewhere. He pulled the sheets from the bed. The plastic wrap beneath too, leaving the bare, clean, mattress. He stuffed a bin liner with the soiled sheets, the plastic. Her clothes. He took it straight downstairs. Put it by the back door and looked out the window to the sky.

Didn't look like rain.

Good.

He was still naked. Blood dried on his skin. Black mixed with his salt and pepper body hair. His hands dark like they were gloved. He went to the bathroom. Showered. Cleaned the night's antics from his body and watched as the girl's juices slid down into the plughole. At least he didn't have to worry about her taking the morning after pill. He dried. Dressed. White work t-shirt. Had paint stains on it. Once black jeans, now faded. Out into the back garden.

Gone ten in the morning, and most of his neighbours would be at work. The perfect time to do some *lawn work*. Owen went to the shed and pulled out the incinerator. An old metal dustbin with a chimney lid. He got the bin liner from the house and emptied the sheets, her clothes, and the plastic into it. It was going to stink for an hour, but that didn't matter.

No one to smell it.

Not if it was done by lunch.

He wouldn't even stick around himself. Errands to run.

Owen got an old local newspaper from the house and scrunched several sheets up, pushing them into the bin with the bloody sheets. Then he took some actual grass cuttings from the lawnmower, dropped those on top and lit it.

He waited until he was sure the flame had taken and then placed the lid on.

Back into the house.

Pulled the tarp down the stairs. He went out the front of the house. He could smell the fire in the back garden. Good. Smelt like burning leaves and plastic. Covered the smell of the blood. No one would know. Care, even. He walked to the front gate and pulled it open. Looked up and down the street. No one.

Perfect.

Owen returned to the house and picked up the tarp. Put it over his shoulder. She was light. Easy to manipulate.

Went to the car. Plucking the fob from his pocket he unlocked it as he approached and popped the boot with his toe. Like he'd done before. Sometimes when he was carrying his shopping. The boot was empty. In preparation.

He dumped the body in. Made a hollow thud as it landed on the floor. Closed the lid.

Murder was easy. Getting rid of the body was easy.

Just act natural and nobody cared.

He returned to the house. Got his jacket. Locked

up. Smelt the smoke from the fire in the garden as he walked down the path. Most of the evidence would already be gone. Got in. Drove away.

Like she was never there.

Owen shopped at a small garden centre. He was buying rocks, for his *rockery*. A couple of new tarps. Yes, he *was* going through them, he would tell them. Working in his allotments. He said whatever he wanted. Different garden centres rotated. No one would ever know what he was buying or why. Paid cash.

Tarps. Rocks. He needed couple of hefty ones the size of a football for the girl. Some rope. Bungies. Grass seed—actually for his back garden—and firelighters. Barbeque season was coming up. Best be prepared. See. You could say anything.

He loaded the back seat of his car. No one cared why none of it was going in the boot. Then he left. Drove out of the town. Onto the dual carriageway. About five miles.

There was a nature reserve that had recently closed, a couple of years back. Everyone was laid off. There was a big furore about it in the local news. What was going to happen to it? Apparently no cared about that in the long run, either. It was in an old quarry, with main roads on either side. It could rot. The staff got other jobs and the nature lovers moved on to the next calamity.

It was vandalised pretty quickly.

No security.

The gates broken open. Left like it.

Owen found you could drive in. If you looked like you were supposed to be there. Nobody cared. Nobody paid attention. And when someone on the news said there was a missing girl in the local town, nobody said, *'ere, you remember when we drove by that old nature reserve? We saw a car driving in there. Very suspicious.*

He parked up in the last parking space before the edge of the quarry. There were beer cans and dog-ends. Joint butts. Kids out there partying at night, probably. He expected someone was probably saying it was haunted by now. He opened the boot of the car and dragged the tarp out. To the edge. Overlooking the lake below. Thriving with life. He looked at the body in the tarp. Well, not all of it was thriving. He unrolled the plastic, the ... human sausage roll. The girl, naked inside. He got the rocks out of the car. Put one in each end of her mock-up coffin, and then re-wrapped and re-tied. He rolled her off the edge.

Then she was gone.

He tried, like he always did, to see if he could see her in the water, but it was far too steep, and far too dangerous. Then he was free to get back in the car. Take the rest of the stuff he'd bought home, for next time. Probably keep the spare tarps and such in the shed. Maybe leave the rocks in the boot, save hefting them about.

See.

Murder is easy.

CHAPTER 5

Owen looked over at the shit on the floor of the toilet cubicle. He was probably going to have to clean that up later, but no one had seen it yet. He'd just leave it. Maybe one of the others would clean it up. It wasn't very likely, but he didn't want to volunteer. He pulled at the waistcoat that was slightly too tight around his belly. Made him feel self-conscious. And he didn't like the company colours, either.

That didn't help.

He put his cock in his trousers and zipped them up. Didn't bother washing his hands. He could feel a dribble of piss there, so he just rubbed his fingers together. You know. Until it just disappeared. Gave his hand a quick sniff before he opened the door.

Back into the supermarket.

The toilets were over in the corner. You had to walk past the security station, and customer service, and almost to the entrance to the café, before you got to them. Hid them away, while discouraging people from using them without shopping. Owen glanced over to the girl working the cigarette kiosk. Pretty thing. Young. Fairly new. Her name was Kiki. At least, that was what her name tag said. Might not have been that. It wasn't like they'd spoken more than a passing *hello, good morning, you okay?*—no reply. She noticed him looking. He looked away. Pulled at his waistcoat. Fucking green.

Strode with purpose towards the door.

At least tried to look like he had some pride in his job.

Opposite the doors to the outside world was the fruit and veg section. Always a bustle of people. Ignorant arsehats. He wiped his hand on his trouser leg, palm down, before stooping and picking up an escapee lemon. Put it back in the green plastic container full of loose lemons. With his piss hand. Someone was going to grate that rind into their salad dressing tonight. Piss lemon salad dressing. He smiled to himself, turning hard right and out the doors into the car park.

Quick nod at the security guard, sitting on a bar stool watching the monitors.

It was chilly out. Owen rolled his shoulders. Side stepped the customers hurrying in from the November weather. Wrapped in coats. Umbrellas collapsed and down like canes. Clacking on the paving. Tripping hazards.

The cold didn't bother him. He walked out, from under the covering of the entrance and straight across the car park. Ever since some bigwig somewhere had decided that it was a good idea to put coin holders on the trollies, it had become easier to collect them. People actually took their trollies back to the collection points in the car park instead of dumping them in empty parking spaces. Owen thought it was just common fucking courtesy to put them back, but no. People were arsehats. Still, even with the one pound to release the trolley, people still managed to leave them scattered around the car park.

He walked over to the first, sitting in the disabled spaces. Took it like he was going to shop and glanced around for the next one. Over the far side. He spotted one up against the hedges. Started pushing the first one towards it. He didn't dislike the job. It paid the bills. The bills were small. He was smart enough to get on the property ladder just after leaving school. Didn't leave him much to worry about these days. So he pushed his trollies across the car park. At least he didn't have to interact with the arsehats.

For the most part.

Speaking of. One was approaching. Had their trolley. Pushing it towards him. There was always one. Thought they were doing you some favour by giving you another trolley to push around. They had no idea how hard it was to steer these things once there were five or six of them. Some bloke. Young. Late twenties. Grinning. He said *It's all right. There's no coin in it.* Like that made a difference. Owen nodded. Smiled thinly. He took the trolley and put it on the front of the first. The man walked away. Owen was closer to his car than the trolley park. Obviously. Still, he could have left the fucking thing in the empty parking space next to the one his car was in.

Owen pushed the two trollies over to the edge of the car park, to the hedge. The one pushed up against the hedge still had the pound in the little lock thing. Owen attached it to the other two trollies and slid the locking mechanisms together. The pound popped out. He pocketed it. Looked at the distance to the nearest trolley park. It was about thirty metres. Who wouldn't walk thirty metres for a pound? More money than sense, some people.

He screwed his nose up.

Arsehats.

CHAPTER 6

Owen sat on the bench that was supposed to be for looking out over the sea. He was sat on the edge of it, so he could see behind it. To the club. Shitty place. Absolutely *banging* tonight as the kids would say.

It had been a week since he'd been there.

Time to try again.

He stood. Brushed down his suit. Slim fit. Perfect fit. Black. White shirt underneath. Collar and one button open. Expensive looking watch on his wrist.

Lies.

Lies and pretence.

Owen walked over the grass towards the doors of the club. It was Friday night. Always the busiest night. Always full of people of all ages. Mostly looking for the same things. The same things he was. At least, that was what *they* thought.

He got to the door.

Most clubs had a line outside. This one didn't even have a doorman most of the time. Sometimes there was a guy called Tony. Tonight there was not. That suited him just fine. He filed in behind everyone else. It was ten. Fairly early. But there were people already going in the other direction. Some people already paired up. Going to fuck. Some leaving with a disdainful look on their face like they'd gone into the place thinking it was a rosette winning restaurant. Not a sweaty flesh market.

Place had a terrible reputation, but as long as you were out before midnight, you never saw the law. They'd turn up when a fight started, usually at closing when some whore didn't want some other john and was hiding in the bogs. Security—Tony—couldn't handle it, or couldn't be found. Might have been drunk somewhere. Might have been getting a twenty-pound blowjob and scabies. The happy meal, as Owen had named it.

He headed straight to the bar. There were four types of people at this hour. Always. The first were like him. Older gentlemen looking for something young and tender. Something quick, and easy. There were the older women—cougars, be believed was the term—looking for the younger, fitter men. There were the young men, and the desirable young women. Twenty five and under. Everybody had their own taste. Desire. Need to be filled. Owen couldn't speak for the rest of them, but he was looking for someone ripe. Inexperienced. Someone who would be impressed with the thought of him having a certain level in society. Someone who might think more about him being a daddy figure—if he had that term right—than a one night stand. Hence the way he dressed and the way he would act. He also liked that those sort of very young women generally couldn't tell the difference between a thousand pound watch, and one from Wish.com.

At the bar, he slid on the stool. Arse half on and half off. It afforded him the ability to look around the club without straining, but also gave him a relaxed air. He didn't like handling the cash in the club, not when it was so busy and Tony was nowhere to be seen—so, basically, most of the time—but it was a necessity. He pulled out his money. It was a couple of hundred in fives. A couple of twenties around the outside. He took one of the twenties and held it out on the bar. Got the attention of the bartender. It was also a signal, he'd learned quite quickly. Some beacon that attracted the right—or wrong, depending on how you looked at it—girls. He ordered a light beer. Something he could nurse for an hour or more without feeling it.

The bartender brought it.

Owen could see a couple of the young girl's interest pique. They were hovering like seagulls over a car in the car park of Burger King. Waiting to strike. The stool next to him was available for whichever one wanted a shot first. He was in control. He had the power. He was the desirable object in this little game, and he wasn't fussed about which one of the girls wanted to have a go first. He rarely turned down the first. It was quite often the youngest. The most impetuous. Someone who had arrived too early in the evening and had drunk too much. Someone whose friends were too young and inexperienced to have a code set up. One where no one left with a handsome stranger alone.

He waited.

Felt empowering. A flytrap for virginal young flesh. The stink of youth, looking for a good time with an older, richer, experienced man.

Then the stool was taken.

Owen didn't look at the girl for a moment or two. Power play. He waited until they were getting impatient. Made him more irresistible when he *was* available.

One minute.

She was tall-ish. He could see from the corner of

his eye. Wearing dark clothes. Not that it mattered. Couldn't tell what she looked like. Sip of beer. Quick glance.

Two minutes.

He looked at her, smiling. Kept his powerful demeanour. He was in charge. He was making the decisions. He was choosing.

She was staring at him already. He had her, if he wanted her. The game was done before she had even realised they were playing.

Oh. She was older than his usual type. Maybe late twenties judging by the look. Um. Huh. What now?

"You buying?" she asked, waving her empty glass at him.

Owen nodded, off kilter. His balance—his balance of power—shaken. "Of course." He focussed on not blowing his cover. His lie. He took the roll of notes, slipped one off, and held it in his hand. Tapped the bar with a single finger.

It couldn't be heard in the bar. Fuck it. Nothing could *really* be heard in the bar, but it was a sign. It said that everybody was watching him because he was more important than everyone else. He was the one that mattered. He was in charge.

CHAPTER 7

Emma slipped on the barstool, slipping forward, slightly, her vodka tonic glass clunking on the edge of the bar. Owen smiled. She was being just as easy as everyone else had been in the past. She leant forward, and slid her drink onto the bar, resting both her hands on it, seemingly to steady herself. He reached forward and patted the back of her hand gently with his own. A warm gesture. One reminiscent of fatherly.

Practiced.

"I think you've had enough," he said quietly. Just loud enough to be heard over the racket of the club between the thumping shitty music. He didn't want to call it songs. It was barely music. But needs must. Owen's eyes ran lightly over Emma. She was wearing a leather jacket. Had a tank top vest thing on underneath. Jeans. She looked like a seventies punk type. Not the usual clientele that the club had—certainly not the sort he usually went for—but what the hell.

A change is as good as a rest.

That's what they say, isn't it? He ran his fingers gently over the skin on the back of her hand. "Can I take you home?" It was a carefully crafted question, designed for a girl in the state that this one was in. Something that could be taken two ways, often was, and easily flipped in speech. The home she was going to return to was a transgression on his part. It was all a misunderstanding.

"Fuck yes," she said. Emma pushed her hand from the bar, sliding out from under his skin, and jammed it into her long brown hair. It was a pretty mess before she did it, more so after. Owen didn't object. He glanced down the bar to the bar staff. There were three of them. The bar was busy, but as always, Owen had conducted his business there. It was the best place for him to get what he needed. He knew that Emma was hitting the drink hard, and had stopped buying about thirty minutes ago. It was nearly eleven thirty now. Time to leave. He'd been ordering her doubles. Triples. And once to a state, stopped ordering as the club had gotten busier. The bar staff had long forgotten him. Her. *Them*. He dropped from the stool to the floor.

"I need a piss first," she said. She waved in the direction of the toilets.

Damn it. Owen smiled. He led her across to the doors to the ladies and waited outside for her. Didn't like it. Too obvious. His immediate reaction was to abort. Give the night up and leave while she was in there. But he wanted to try her. He wanted to know.

She returned quickly.

Wiped her face with the back of her leather. Sniffing. Like she'd done a line of something, like they do in the movies. Probably nothing. She staggered by, into the crowd of people, ignoring him at first, and then calling back. "Well, come on then."

In the back of his mind there was still the nagging thought that he should give it up. Flee. She wasn't worth it. But the devil on his shoulder was telling him that she was. She was prettier than the girls he normally picked up. She had grown to beauty, rather than those young slip of a thing girls, barely pubescent. Maybe that was what he needed. Someone older and more experienced. He drew a thin smile and followed her across the club towards the exit. Watched as her arse moved in her jeans. Tight. She had a big arse. He liked that. Usually got it too. She glanced over her shoulder to him. He raised his hand to gesture that he was still there.

To the door.

She was already outside having pushed by the people coming in. Waiting in the cold night air. Owen rolled his shoulders. Too much time sitting at the bar didn't do his joints any good. Emma pulled a pack of fags from her pocket and waved them at him. Owen put his hand up as a no, annoyed slightly that she smoked. He didn't like the smell on him. Or her. It would be on her clothes. He hadn't smelt it in the club. Maybe she didn't smoke much? She pulled one from the pack and lit it. She coughed.

Owen waved her towards the road. "I'm parked over there."

She nodded and came up next to him. "Fucking hell." She weaved a little and then grabbed onto his arm, steadying herself. "Fresh air and nicotine. Doubles the impact."

"Quite," Owen replied. He liked that she was gone enough to hold onto him. He liked her warmth. She slipped her hand into his and squeezed. There was something about it. Something attractive … welcoming … he couldn't quite put his finger on it. There was something about her. To the road, onto the path and along. About a hundred metres from the club and to his car. He pressed the button on the fob. The car beeped, and he opened the passenger door for her.

"Gentleman," she said. She flopped into the car.

The weight off her legs. Struggling, it appeared, to stay upright.

Good. He closed the door and went around to the driver's side. Got in. Stuck the keys in the ignition. Started the car. There was a *bing* from the dash. He looked at the lights. Seatbelt. He turned to her. She still had the cigarette hanging from her mouth. The car was getting smoky. He leant over her, getting his face close to hers. Her eyes met his, but she didn't move. Like he was making a move on her. But she was going to let him. He grabbed the seatbelt and dragged it across her. Clipped it in. She smiled, let out a little laugh. Embarrassment, perhaps. Owen smiled at her, clipped himself in. "Don't want to get in trouble with the police, do we now?" *Don't want to get pulled over. Some plod seeing us together would put an end to the night real quick.*

Emma snorted. "No. Most definitely." She slid her hand into Owen's crouch, smooshed it around a bit and then removed it. She looked out the window for a few minutes without speaking.

Owen drove out of the town. He lived in a smaller village a few miles out. A hamlet of sorts. Had a pub. Not one that he could pick up women in. And a post office-village store. That was about it. That and some houses. Well. A lot of houses anyway. There was a thud when Owen went around the roundabout towards the village as Emma banged her head on the window.

She made a light grunting sound, but still didn't speak.

Two shades to the wind. Owen smiled. He turned into the village and straight through into the built up area on the other side. Into the cul-de-sac. It was usually about there that the question was raised. *Where are we? This isn't where I live.* Oh, he would say. When I said take you home ... his voice would drop away. A little disappointment hinted at. Then he would ask if they wanted to come in for a coffee. Something like that. Depended on the girl. Then he could take them home. After. Once inside, the rest, as they say, would be history.

"We gonna fuck?" Emma suddenly said.

It was such a surprise that Owen nearly swerved the car. "Do you want to?" he asked, quietly. He wasn't used to this approach. They were usually younger. Timid.

"Why not?" She pointed out the window like a baby. "Which one is yours?"

Owen pulled up, into the driveway of the house. "This one."

She looked out the front window to the house. "Ah." She opened the door. Struggled to get out. Realised she was still clipped in. Owen released the seatbelt. She nearly fell out onto the drive. Managed to get her feet. She seemed to be getting worse. The fresh air really did get to her. Owen shook his head lightly. Better get her in the house before she started making a noise. She could make noise once she was inside.

He got out. Went around to her side of the car and took her arm. Guided her towards the house. "Cool," she mumbled. Owen leaned her against the front door and opened up. Led her in. Closed the door.

Safe at last.

CHAPTER 8

Emma went to the sofa. Wobbly, but made it. She sat down. Knees closed. Ankles apart. Made her look like a punk baby doe. She pinched her nose like she was trying not to sneeze. "Got any wine?" she asked.

Owen grinned. She *was* different. He nodded. "White?" He asked it as a question, but she was getting white. He already had a bottle in the fridge. He was around the stairs and to the door of the kitchen before she spoke again.

"Do you mind if I smoke?"

"I would prefer it if you—"

"Thanks."

Owen went into the kitchen and hung his head a little. He was going to have to get rid of that smell now, too. Still. She was probably going to be worth the extra trouble. He opened the fridge. His hand wavered over the good stuff, and then he grasped the Aldi bottle. Two glasses chinked together as he lifted them from the shelf and took them back to the living room. She was flicking cigarette ash into her hand. Owen put the wine and glasses down. "I'll, er," his words drifted off as he gestured back towards the kitchen once again.

Back in there he looked around for something for her to use as an ashtray. Owen picked up a saucer from the draining board and took it back with him. Placed it on the table as he started to open the wine. Get this thing started.

His focus on the bottle, Owen glanced up to his guest. She was watching him intently. Eyes piercing.

"You've done this before," she said. Matter-of-factly. Words slurred.

Owen nodded. Wasn't about to hide it.

She stubbed out the cigarette, and sat back on the sofa. Looking up at the ceiling. "Want to do me in here?" She snorted lightly. "Or the bedroom."

"Wherever you'd like," Owen replied. It really didn't matter to him where they started. It always ended in the bedroom. He poured two glasses of wine. Two hefty ones. He could enjoy himself now. Not just watch her drink, but he could partake too. He lifted hers, passing it to her.

She took it.

Graciously. Most of them took it with some surprise, like they weren't used to the chase. Well, not this sort of chase, anyway. It was like they were expecting him to have tried to slip it up their arse already. But this time it was different. Maybe he'd been playing the game wrong himself all this time. Maybe he should have been going for someone a little older. More mature. Someone like this. He was licking his lips as he thought. Staring at her.

And she was watching him over the lip of her glass. She smiled. Slid forward on the sofa. A little unsteady. She placed the glass down on the coffee table. Put her hand on his knee. Kissed him on the lips. Gently. Seductively. Owen responded. Kissed her back. Harder. Then she pulled away. Put her finger up onto his lip. Touching the bottom one. "Hold up," she said. Emma stood. She slipped the leather jacket off her shoulders and then dropped it behind her, catching it, and pulling it back around in front of her jeans. She had ink across her shoulders.

He'd never had a girl with tattoos before. "I need a piss first," she said.

Owen blinked frantically like he'd just been woken up. "Oh, um. Yes. Of course." He smiled at her.

Emma shook her head. Eyebrows went up. "Where is it?" she asked quietly.

"Oh. Top of the stairs. Door opposite."

She grinned. "Good boy," she said. She turned away, staggered over to the stairs and started up, dragging her jacket behind her. She was focussing on the stairs. Not on him.

Owen picked up his glass of wine and took a sip. He heard the bathroom door go at the top of the stairs. Admiring the clear light yellow liquid in the bottle, Owen changed his mind and gulped down the rest of the glass. Placed the empty down on the table and refilled it.

Toilet flush.

He stood. Paced around the sofa. He unbuttoned his suit jacket, let it fall open. Not bad. No. He took it off. Draped it over the armchair, before sitting back down on the sofa. She was still up there. What was she doing? Lady things, probably. It always amused Owen at how long it took the girls to pee. He could hear her moving about in the bathroom. Floor boards creaking. Never bothered him when he was there on his own. Really needed to get someone in to look at it though.

What was she doing?

Poking around, he expected. She wouldn't find much. A few vitamin bottles. That sort of thing. Nothing incriminating. He smiled to himself. Not up there, anyway.

Door to the bathroom re-opened.

She started down the stairs.

Owen picked up his glass and sipped. Gently. Evenly. In control. He was in control. She flopped down on the sofa next to him nearly causing him to spill his drink. "Here," she said. She dropped something in his lap. Owen's eyes dropped down to look. Her knickers. Red. Lacy. *Looking for some action* sort of knickers. He couldn't stifle the grin.

Emma sniffed. Sat back. "Well?" she said. "How hard are you for me?"

It was very forward. Put Owen off his game slightly. He was more used to having to woo a frightened little whore, sometimes having realised she'd gotten way out of her depth. He breathed in deep. Maintained composure. "Wouldn't you like to know?" He looked at her out of the side of his eye. Stayed in control. He turned slightly. So he could see her. Without the leather jacket on he could see the shape of her body. It was better shaped than the younger girls barely able to bleed yet. They hadn't toned their bodies. They were just milky, fleshy, babies. She had muscle. Used to exercising. Should be a different experience. He kept back. Held his distance. "Why don't you let me see you?"

CHAPTER 9

Emma chuckled lightly, pulling herself to the edge of the sofa. Pushed herself up to stand. Over him. She unfastened the button on her jeans but didn't do anything more. Her finger slipped into the dip of the neck of her vest, and she pulled it down a little.

Owen controlled his breath. Didn't want to get too excited. He could see her play though. Power move. She wanted to be in control, too. It was going to be an interesting night.

She sat back down, quickly. Loosely. Like her muscles didn't work properly. Bent forward. Unzipped the side of her boot and pushed it off. Then the other. She had stockings on under there. Under the denim.

Owen licked his lips. He noted that they were quivering slightly. He *should* have gone for an older woman the whole time. Sure, there was more risk that she'd be missed. That she might fight back. But the rewards …

Emma stumbled to a stand again. She moved around in front of Owen like the lap dancers he'd seen on the Segal movies. Then she raised her foot up and plonked it into his groin. It was supposed to be sexy—he guessed—but her lack of balance meant she'd done it too hard. He grunted out of discomfort, and she said something along the lines of *yeah, you like that don't you?* He wasn't really listening. More focussed on the warmth of his testicles. She proceeded to rub his cock with her stockinged foot. He supposed if she wasn't so drunk it *might* actually have done something for him.

Then she dragged the vest up over her head. Chucked it across the room. She had a bra on underneath that might have matched the knickers that were still in his hand. He raised them to his face and sniffed them. Didn't even think about it. Just wanted to. It raised a little laugh from her. He glanced from them to her. She was staring down on him. In control. She was running the show.

Shit. Owen tossed them to the side and took her ankle in his grip pushing her foot out from his crotch, and letting it drop to the floor.

"Oh, I see," she said. The *ee* in see was elongated, and Owen didn't think it was on purpose. "Like that is it?"

Owen grunted an affirmation. Yes. It was. He stood. His face in hers. Kissed her lips. A quick pushing nip. Tease. She went to put her arms around him and he stopped her. He turned the two of them around so she had her back to the sofa. He pushed himself against her, and reached around behind her. Unclipped her bra. Then as he slipped away from her, pulled it with him. She looked down at herself. "Nice," she said. Approval of the move. Owen dropped the undergarment between them and then pushed her—hard enough to assert dominance—back onto the sofa. She dropped with ease, barely able to stand anyway. "Oi, oi," she said, reaching forward towards his trousers, now at her face height.

Owen pushed her hands away. "No," he snapped. "Bad girl."

Emma grinned, put her forefinger in between her lips and chewed on it. "Okay, Daddy," she said.

Better. Owen slowly unbuttoned his shirt. He was looking down on her. She had tattoos on her stomach. On her breasts. He wasn't close enough to see what they were. Some pictures. Some writing. He might check them out later, maybe not. She was watching him. One finger in her mouth, the other turning circles on one of her nipples.

Owen pulled his shirt off.

"Cock," she said. "I want cock."

"All in good time." He dropped his hand down for her to take. When she did, he pulled her up to standing again. Kissed her hard. Turned her around so she was facing away from him. Ran his hands across her stomach. Up to her breasts. He was surprised that he couldn't *feel* the tattoos. He expected them to feel different somehow. She reached around. Behind herself. Both her hands around her arse, the front of his trousers. She was messing. Feeling.

"What's up?" she said. She pushed away from him slightly, almost overbalancing and falling back onto the sofa. Turned back to face him and grabbed his cock. Gently squishing. "Need some more encouragement, eh?" She dropped to her knees and undid his belt. Opened his trousers.

Owen let her. She was stronger than he was used to. He wanted her. He wanted her so much. She was toying with his cock. Soft. Flaccid. Dead.

Like always.

"Do you need a blue pill or something," she said before enveloping his skin with her mouth.

The warmth was amazing. The feeling indescribable. Owen put his hand on her head, let his fingers entwine her hair. Help move her back and forth. But it wasn't making a difference. She let him go, pulling back. She shuffled backwards onto the sofa and pulled her jeans down, off her hips and over her knees. To her ankles. Stood, naked in front of him. "You want me," she said. It was an order.

And he did.

But nothing was happening. It never did.

She pulled him as she dropped back onto the sofa. Drawing him down onto her. "Fuck me," she whispered. "*Fuck me*." The second time more urgent.

Owen fiddled with his cock now. Trying to make it work. So frustrating. Why did it happen every time? He stared onto her body. At her beautiful body. Wanted her so much. Closer now, he could see tattoos better. He was sure he should have been able to decipher them from standing—maybe he needed new glasses? There was a picture of a devil. Cute little one. And a heart. It wasn't so cute. Animorphically correct? No ... that wasn't the word. And some writing.

This isn't helping.

She slid up, away from his touch a little. "What's wrong?" she asked. "You do want me, don't you?"

"Yes, yes," he muttered. "I ..." his words fading away. He stopped struggling. Let his hand drop away from his cock.

"Look." She righted herself on the sofa. "I need a piss again." She nodded down herself. "Small bladder. Runs in the family. We'll try again when I get back." She stood. Took her jacket and nothing else and went upstairs.

Owen rolled over onto his back and stared down at his dead, useless, dick. "Shit," he muttered.

Thought this time would be different. He kicked his trousers and pants off to the floor. Sat there naked apart from his socks.

Toilet flush.

She didn't return again straight away. Like she was poking around again. Maybe she was looking for some *blue pills*. Shit. Owen let out a long sigh before she returned down the stairs. Jacket was gone. Must have left it in the loo. He turned to face her and she came, sat next to him. Legs spread. Unabashed. "So," she said quietly. "Let see if we can't start the motor." Her fingers were between her legs. Stroking herself. Like she couldn't be bothered to wait for him to get on with it.

He looked at her chest. *Kooky Cultist* were the words above the heart. *Anatomically* correct. That was it. He pointed at the words below the heart. Touching her skin lightly. "What does that say?" he asked quietly. Maybe if he let the moment take him something might happen.

"It's Latin," she replied. "They're evocation tats."

"What's that?"

"Never mind," she said. She stopped fingering herself. "This isn't working, is it?" She swung her legs out, off the sofa, and stopped. Wavering. Like she'd been hit by drink again. Harder now. She leaned forward and picked up her wine. Steadied herself on the table. "Fucking bollocks," she muttered.

"Don't you think you've had enough?" he said.

She repeated the words back to him, mocking. "No," she said. "Apparently I'm not getting anywhere tonight." She looked at him.

Owen had screwed his face up. How dare she?

"Look," she continued. "I've had a good time, yeah. It's not your fault. I take it you don't have anything medical that will help." Her voice was badly slurred. She was looking around for her underwear. Maybe. It was hard to tell. She was unsteady. Very unsteady.

Owen stood, and she ignored him. Still gazing around, a little glassy eyed.

"Cunt," she said under her breath to no one and at nothing.

Owen stood there, just behind her. "Don't get dressed," he said. "Come up to bed. Let's try one more time."

She looked at him. There was something behind her eyes. He couldn't tell if it was pity there or what. "I'm ... not in the mood ... now." She held her hand to her forehead. "Burning," she muttered. "Maybe next time."

God damn it. Owen took her by the shoulders. Turned her around. "No," he snapped at her. "You can't leave now. I don't want you to."

She slapped at his arms, trying to get him to release his grip but was nowhere near strong enough. "What are you doing. Calm ... it. I'll get a cab." She continued to struggle weakly. "No need to lose your shit over it."

No. Owen released her enough to grab her arm and drag her down onto the sofa. She yelled out as he yanked her, pulling her down. She said something that had the words *fuck* and *doing* in amidst some other words he couldn't make out, before he had his fingers on her throat.

Squeezing.

"Calm down, Zoe," he said. "Calm down." She stopped struggling almost instantly. Her throat convulsed, white putrid gloop dribbled out of her mouth. He'd only gripped her for a few seconds. She couldn't have had the life squeezed from her yet. "Come on, Zoe," he said. "Let's go to bed."

"Who's Zoe?" *Click. Click. Click.*

Owen jumped out of his skin, turning to the voice coming from behind him. It was her. Sitting in the armchair. Flicking a lighter. Lighting a cigarette. He looked down at the body beneath him. Her. Back to the … her … on the chair. His heart started to thump erratically.

Owen grabbed his chest.

CHAPTER 10

"Calm down, old man." She grinned at him. Naked bar stockings. Sitting there, legs spread. Cigarette in her mouth. "No need to have a heart attack."

Owen crawled back over the corpse on the sofa. His face contorted into some bizarre gurn. Horror in his eyes. "Who ... who ..." he was saying over and over. He pointed at Emma like she was an apparition.

She blew smoke out, between the two of them and stood. Stubbed out the cigarette on the coffee table. She slapped her pubic mound and stepped over to Owen. He was half laying on Emma's corpse and half on the sofa. Breathing hard. His heart fast. Settled, at least, into a rhythm. Like trance music or some shit. Emma leaned down ignoring him, and looking at the corpse. "Oh dear," she said. "I could feel it coming." She glanced at Owen.

Owen was staring at her. He could feel the corpse *her* beneath him. Still warm. Clammy. He shuffled away from the other *her*. The one standing up. This was so confusing. "What are you?"

Emma looked from the corpse to Owen and back again. "Her. Isn't that obvious?" She stood and looked down at her naked self. A corpse in stockings. Bobbed her head from side to side admiring her. Herself. Whatever. "I don't look that different, do I?" Now she looked down at herself. Her standing herself. Poked at her titty. Ran her fingers down the sides of her body. "Everything seems to be in place." She turned to Owen. "What's the problem?"

Owen screamed. "Jesus, Lord our Christ. Get out

of my house."

Emma looked around, then placed her hand on her chest, flat. "Moi?" She shook her head. "Oh, no. I've got so many questions."

"You've got questions?" he blurted. "*You've* got questions?"

"Yes," she nodded. "Yes I have." She stepped out of the way of both the corpse and Owen. Returned to the armchair and then sat. Crossed her legs. Like a bloke.

Owen could see her taint clearly. It was like she didn't care. He then looked back to the corpse. "What happened?" he asked quietly. Then he puked. Couldn't help it. Didn't even feel it coming. The wine. And the low alcohol crap from the club. Spewed out of him like a sprinkler. He didn't even have time to prepare. Went everywhere. Over the table. Over the corpse. The carpet. Sofa.

When he stopped, Emma started clapping. "Holy shit," she said. "Do it again."

Owen covered his mouth with his hand and sat there. Half on and half off the sofa now. Facing the … other girl. His senses being attacked by the stank of bile. He let out a little whimper. Belched. Tasted like puke.

"Oh, come on," she said. "Get it together. You haven't got all night."

"What do you mean?" His voice was no louder than a whisper.

"Well, if you hadn't worked it out, I'm not, well, me anymore." She gestured to the corpse. "But that's all the information I'm prepared to give you at the moment. I want some answers from you. Or there'll be trouble." She uncrossed her legs, drawing Owen's gaze. "And you can forget that too. *I* am not in the mood any longer."

Owen shook his head. Kept shaking it. "No. I didn't do anything." He looked at the corpse as if to say *it was like that when I got here*.

Emma stood, walked over to the body and looked down on it. Sniffed it, weirdly. "Oddly enough, no, you didn't kill me." She turned back and hunted around for her underwear. Found the knickers. Slid them back on. "O.D.," she said. Shrugged. "Bound to happen one day." She slumped back onto the armchair. Flicked her nipple absently. "So who's Zoe?"

Owen was still shaking his head. Hadn't stopped. Absolutely dumbfounded. Looked at the body again. "Doesn't matter," he said, quietly.

"Can't get it up?"

His head shook. He was still vehemently denying everything rather than answering this ... ghost's ... questions.

He looked back to her. The one that was talking. "Who are you?" he asked. He was suddenly aware of his nakedness. "What do you want? Did ... God ... send you?"

Emma looked down at herself and snorted. "Do I look like an angel, motherfucker?" She nodded at the body. "How you gonna get rid of me?"

Owen focused back on the corpse. This was all a figment of his imagination, brought on by stress. Had to be. Yes. The figment had a good idea. Focus on getting rid of the body. "I'm just going to get dressed," he said to himself. "Then I'm going to take the body to the quarry and ditch it." He nodded to himself. Pretend she—it—wasn't there. Owen stood and started to faff, getting his clothes together, but not dressing. "Yes," he said quietly. Ignoringly. "That is what I will do." He couldn't help but glance at her.

"Still here, bitch," she said.

Owen looked at her, snatching his glare away just as quickly as it landed.

"You can't just ignore me."

Owen could. Would. It wasn't real and he was going to treat it as such. He picked up his wine. Took a gulp. Emptied the glass—again. He refilled it, still having the pile of clothes in his other arm, before taking it and the clothes up the stairs. Took a deep breath. Everything was fine. Normal. *Absolutely normal*.

Fine.

CHAPTER 11

Owen showered quickly before hitting the hay. He was tired. Long day. Lots to do tomorrow. Had to trip to the quarry. Had everything he needed for that. Maybe go to a café after. Treat himself to a nice coffee. One of those fancy ones. Something with a shot of something in. He rubbed himself down. He'd rather unusually closed the bathroom door. The house was empty. The house was *always* empty. But he'd closed the bathroom door.

Made him feel better.

After his episode.

He hung the towel over the radiator, and pulled the pants on he'd brought in with him. He liked to sleep in y-fronts. Felt supporting. But naked other than that. Tonight was no different. Her leather jacket was pushed hard into the corner of the bathroom by the cabinet. He picked it up, opened the door. Held his breath subconsciously as he did. But she wasn't there. On the landing.

Of course she wasn't. None of it was real, was it? He smiled to himself. Out the bathroom. Tossed her jacket to the floor. He could see down the stairs from where he stood. Not all of it. Just a little. Enough to see the corpse on the sofa. It was going to have to stay there for the night. He was too tired to go back downstairs now. He'd put the wine on the bedside table and was going to drink it while he read a book. Something to relax him. Steady his nerves. Obviously today had gotten the better of him.

He wandered down to the bedroom. Dumped his

dirty clothes on the floor by the armchair he had in the corner. For reading. He usually preferred to read in bed these days.

He slid under the cool sheet. It caressed his cold, clammy skin. Pushed the pillow against the headboard and sat against it. Picked up the book from the nightstand. It was a cosy mystery. *Paris saves Paris*, it was called. An elderly woman and her crime busting dog called Paris who had gone on holiday to Paris from England, and stumbled across a murder, getting all involved with the gendarmes. Very *Murder, She Wrote*. Except you couldn't take a dog abroad to France now without quarantine. Leaving the EU and all that. But how believable was a book about a crime busting old lady and a dog supposed to be?

He opened the book to the page bookmarked, and rested it on his knees. Took a sip of wine. Placed the glass down. "Now where was I?" he muttered, looking at the page. His memory was getting worse these days. He was sure of it.

His eyes were already getting tired.

―

Owen struggled to breathe. He felt a tightness in his chest. His eyes fluttered open, trying to get used to the darkness in the room. He didn't remember turning the light off. Must have been half asleep. Maybe he'd finished the wine. Why couldn't he get a breath?

"Why?" Emma screamed into his face. She was there, encompassing his vision. Her face. Contorted. Angry. Hate.

Owen screamed. Tried to move. Couldn't. She was straddled across him. Knees either side of his body, holding his arms to his side.

"Why did you try to kill me?"

His teeth grit together. Owen could feel tears rising in his eyes. They weren't tears of sadness, but anger. She had no right to do this. She wasn't real.

Emma rose up, over him, on him like they were fucking. Fucking like lovers. She was still naked from the waist up. He couldn't see anything below that. She punched her hand up into the air, clawed, and then thrust it down, down onto Owen.

Into Owen.

Suddenly he could feel her inside him. She'd punctured her way into his chest. He could feel her fingers sliding around his heart. Caressing it. He stared at his chest, wide-eyed. There was no blood, no gore. Her hand just disappeared inside of him like a ghost. "What are you?" he asked. The words barely audible. His face frozen in fear.

Emma's hand surrounded his muscle. Her fingers around it, behind it. She tightened her grip. Not squeezing. Not yet. She just held it there. As it beat. Harder. Faster. Pushing his frightened blood around his veins. She leaned down so that her face was no more than an inch from his, their noses, almost touching, their lips so close. "I am neither one thing nor the other. I belong to the bête noire. My lover is Mephistopheles. Bequeathed to him since I announced my intention …" her voice lowered to a whisper, "… as the kinky cultist whore I am." She started grunting like she was going to cum. There in his face. Grunting, giggling. A huff. Ooh. Aah. Giggle. "And you can't even get it up for me, can you?" Then she started to laugh harder.

Owen's breathing shortened. She was squeezing his heart, stopping it from pumping properly. This was it. He was going to die. Here in bed. A heart attack. Dead slut on the sofa downstairs.

Oh, well.

A calmness came over him. Perhaps it was better like this, than some of the other ways his life might come to an end.

"You're not getting away with it that easily," she said. Emma released his heart and pulled her hand from his body. She shuffled down his torso like a temptress, pulling the sheets from him, baring his body to the night. She lurched forward, grabbed his pants and dragged them away.

Owen tried to stop her, but his effort was half-hearted. Not only was he tired, breathless, and afraid. There was still a small part of him that wanted this to all be a dream. "Please," he whimpered. "Get away from me."

"I will only stop if you tell me who Zoe is." She grinned. Maniacal. She sniffed his pants and tossed them to the side. Ran her fingers down her body while she waited for her answer like she wasn't really listening at all.

Owen didn't want to answer. She didn't seemed to care if he did, so he kept his mouth shut.

Maybe she'd just go away?

Emma looked at him. "Now I'm not human any longer, do you think I should change my name?" She looked him straight in the eye. Waiting. Fingers sliding down into her knickers. Touching herself.

Owen watched. Transfixed.

"For someone who can't get it hard for a pretty

girl, you seem awfully interested." She pulled her fingers out. Tasted them. "So, Zoe? Who is she?"

Owen sighed. Laying naked. His chest hurt. Every time his heart beat he could feel the bruising on it from where she'd touched him. His head dropped down, his chin resting on his chest. He shook it. No. He didn't want to share.

Emma suddenly bound forward. "You will tell me," she hissed. She grabbed his balls in her fist and squeezed. "You will tell me or you *will* fuck me."

Owen screamed out in pain. Beggar the neighbours. If they heard and called the police they'd find the body downstairs. But this would stop. This had to stop. It felt like he'd been kicked in the balls, but the pain didn't stop or subside, or ease, and she twisted, back and forth, a dominatrix he'd never asked for. Paralysed by the pain, he could feel the sickness brewing in him. A vile, bile filled barf that was coming up, whether he wanted it to, or not. He was still laying flat on his back, his body curled as best it could, but she was stopping him, one hand plunged deep between his legs, the other holding his knees apart. He tried to turn to the side. Stop it from coming, but it was in his throat.

Owen's sick rose out of him.

She let go. He was free to roll. Onto his side. Vomit careening out to the sheets. He wailed in pain. Crying. Pleading. *Please*, he was saying, *what do you want?* His face embedded in the sick, he stopped. Waiting as the burning subsided briefly. He looked around the bedroom. She was gone.

CHAPTER 12

Owen screwed his face up. He huffed out some breaths, curled foetal on the bed. His balls hurt. He was obviously losing his mind. "Oh, my Christ," he whispered. He was clenching the sheets in his fist. Had vomit over everything. It all smelt like cheap wine, too. He rolled off the bed, and looked around the room in the darkness. Reached under the lamp and turned it on. He was half expecting to see her standing there. In the shadows.

He padded over to the bedroom door. Stopped. Looked down at his cock. He was naked. He glanced around. His pants were on the floor by the bed. Owen shook his head. Took off onto the landing and into the bathroom. Turned the shower on.

Maybe there was something wrong with him. Delusions. Seeing things. Maybe he should see a doctor. He stepped under the warm water and let it run over his body. Washed off the vomit. His head rested against the wall. He wondered what time it was. Didn't want to sleep anymore.

He got out the shower and barely dried himself off. Thought about watching TV for a while, but when he got to the top of the stairs, he could see the corpse. Laying naked on the sofa. He still didn't know what happened. What *really* happened. He must have strangled her.

Must have.

He looked down at his body. Made the decision to dress. Owen went back into the bedroom. He surveyed the bed. The sheets. The vomit dribbling off everything. Shook his head. Not now. He opened the cabinet and dressed. Pair of pants, clean. Shorts. T-shirt. It was warm enough in the house.

He picked up her leather and went downstairs. Watched the corpse on the sofa—just in case. Kept one eye on the armchair. At the bottom, in the living room, he chucked her jacket onto the armchair. Went to the back of the house. To the kitchen.

He went in.

Ignored that she was sitting on the counter. Legs crossed. Naked apart from stockings and knickers. Just a figment of his imagination.

"Watcha doin'?" she asked.

He glanced at her. It was instinct. A reaction. Then he looked away. Ignore her. She wasn't really there.

"Oi," she barked.

Again. Ignore. Owen started making a cup of tea. He could see out the kitchen window that it was getting lighter. The sun cracking forth from the horizon. Would be light in maybe an hour. That made it what? Four now? That would do. Time to face the day. He switched the kettle on and got a cup and saucer out of the cabinet. He was aware that Emma was sitting on the counter. But she wasn't real.

"Ready to tell me who Zoe is yet?"

Angered, Owen turned. "You're not real," he barked at her.

"Fucking hell," she chirped. "Calm yo tits, old man. I was just asking." She made a clicking noise with her mouth. "So ... you gonna get rid of the body?" He turned away. Back to his tea. Ignored her. "You know, if you were a real man, you'd have fucked me last night. Then none of this would have happened. Is that why you did it?"

The question hung in the air. Ignoring her.

"Probably," she continued, unperturbed. "Can't get it up so take it out on the woman. Man. Badger. Whatever. It's very serial killery." She breathed in, sharp. "You're not a serial killer are you?"

Owen continued to stare at the kettle.

She made an *eep* noise. "Am I in the presence of infamy?"

The kettle clicked and Owen poured his tea. He picked up the cup and saucer and when he turned back, she was gone.

"Jesus wept," he muttered. Taking the tea into the other room. He stood there at the door into the kitchen, looking at the back of the sofa. From there he couldn't see the actual corpse, but he knew it was there. He sat at the dining table in the back of the living room, and looked out the sliding doors into the back garden. There was just enough light that he could make out the shed. Get rid of the body, he thought to himself.

Drinking his tea.

Breathing shallow. Calm. Just get rid of it. Then it'll be done. She'll be gone. Maybe someone older wasn't such a good idea. Maybe try the original plan next time and stick to it. Maybe try a different club. Somewhere out of the town. In the city. It shouldn't take long to find another sleazy outfit within easy driving distance.

CHAPTER 13

Owen rifled through Emma's leather jacket. He was sitting in the armchair with the jacket on his lap. Every now and again he'd glance over to the corpse. The colour had drained out of it now. She was going to be cold to the touch. He pulled out her wallet. Looked at an old university identity card. She was twenty-nine. He glanced over again. Emma Smith. Couldn't get much more generic than that. He ignored the cash in there and pushed the wallet back into the pocket. It wasn't his style to rob the dead. Very gauche. A couple of pockets with rubbish in, McDonald's vouchers. Bus ticket. In the other inside pocket was a bag of white powder. Owen knew little to nothing of drugs. He'd seen films, so he knew that cocaine went up the nose, and heroine went in the arm. He didn't think they were interchangeable, but he could have been wrong about that. It must have been coke. There was no spoon or anything. Needles. He remembered she was sniffing a lot when they left the club. His eyes rested on the baggie for some minutes.

Part of him wanted to know. Wanted to try it. Maybe it would help? Get the old boy up? But he didn't know how much. Or what it was. He looked at the corpse. She'd probably tell me if I asked, but she's only a figment of my imagination, so it would just be my own guess work anyway.

He placed the bag on the coffee table, deciding to keep it. For later. Maybe. Owen stood, collecting up her clothes. He took them to the back garden. Into the bin for burning. No weird smells this time. Dumped some leaves on top that he'd collected from up by the fence the other day.

It was still early. Six in the morning. He'd light it later. Decided to get rid of the body now though. It was best. Get on with it, like. He already had everything he needed from last time. So he'd do it now. Before the work traffic started.

Owen got up and went to the shed. Got the tarp he had stashed there.

Put it on the floor in front of the sofa and rolled the body onto it. The corpse made a grunting sound as it landed. Scared the shit out of him. Then the room filled with the putrid smell of shit. "Jesus," he muttered. He folded the tarp over and tied it. Gave a look around the room. She wasn't there to see. See. She was a figment. He pulled the tarp with the corpse up and struggled to get it over his shoulder. She was heavier than they usually were. Muscle, he suspected.

Heavier than puppy fat.

Owen got her over and took her out to the car. Popped the boot. Dumped the body. Ritual. Quick and easy. He returned to the house.

Dressed himself in something less casual, and then headed out.

To the quarry.

———

He dragged the body out of the boot and lay it on the grass at the edge of the drop. The grass had a dew clinging to it. It was cold. He looked at the tarp, just for that one last second, and then crouched to push.

"Just gonna toss me off?" She laughed. "*Toss me*

off. Get it?" She paused. "No?"

Owen turned his head and looked at Emma, stood on the edge of the quarry, naked apart from knickers and stockings, as she looked over.

"Toss me off," she said again. "Shame I can't say the same for you."

Owen shook his head. All right. We'll do it your way. "Haven't you got any shame? You're not dressed for the outdoors."

Emma looked down at herself. "I put knickers on, didn't I?"

Owen turned his attention back to the tarp. The object in the tarp. "Maybe this'll shut you up." He rolled it off the edge.

Emma watched it go. She turned to him. He was smugly smiling at her, waiting for her to disappear. She strode over to him. Grabbed him by the scruff of his neck and manhandled him to the edge. She had unfathomable strength. Like she was made of steel. He flapped at her arms, where she had a hold of him, but it was like fighting against an unnatural force. She pushed him until his feet barely had any rock beneath them. Holding him so far over the edge that he could see down. See the corpse, splattered on the rocks below, the tarp split open. The young woman's guts spilled out. The stone painted crimson.

"Maybe I should just fucking kill you now?" she said.

"No," Owen blurted. His stomach rolled with the height, as did his head. Swimming. He was never good with heights. He could feel the sweat poke out on his brow. His legs weaken. Shaking.

"Who's Zoe?"

"She was my love. My only love." The words came out wavy. Shaking. No control.

Emma pulled him back to the solidity of the grass. Away from the top of the quarry. "Go on."

Owen looked away, then down. Wouldn't meet her look. He didn't want to say anything. Nothing more.

"Right," she said. She slapped her hands onto his head, like she was going to head butt him. She had the strength of a bear—not that Owen had much experience of wrestling bears.

He could feel her fingers, squeezing his head, as her hands gripped, pushing pressure points on his skull. Then he could feel her fingers sinking into his bone. Her hands sliding into his flesh. His vision started to black. He could feel her beneath his skull. Her skin tickling his brain matter. He tried to speak, but there were no words there. His breathing was short. Sharp. Like he'd forgotten how.

"You know what you need?" she suddenly asked.

Owen couldn't reply. She was inside him. She was part of him. Seeking his secrets. Searching his truths.

She pulled her hands from his head and Owen dropped to his knees. He made a noise like he'd just stood on a hedgehog with nothing on his feet. Air returning to his lungs as he managed to regain some composure. He looked down at himself. He'd pissed. Could feel the warmth. "What?" he whispered hoarsely. "What do you want?"

She knelt down next to him.

"I am not going to leave you, until I can fuck you." She talked in nothing but a whisper. "How does that sound?"

Owen nodded briefly. "I don't know how you think you're going to manage that."

"I've seen inside you."

CHAPTER 14

Owen sat in the car. It was night time. He'd been there for some considerable length of time. Just down the street from some shady looking nightspot in the city. Emma was sitting in the passenger seat. He side-eyed her again.

"It's okay," she cooed. "No one can see me."

"So you keep saying. They can just see me, apparently. Sitting in my motor, watching young girls going into a club in the middle of the evening. I'm sure that makes all the difference."

Emma had a small smile on her face. "I could show myself," she said.

Owen glanced down at her bare flesh. She'd even lost the knickers and stockings in transit somewhere. He shook his head and looked away. "I don't think so." Big sigh. "I just don't see what we're achieving here. What you're achieving. Me."

"You'll see." She suddenly raised her hand and pointed through the window. "Her."

Owen followed the line of her finger to a girl on the other side of the street. She sure looked like she was heading for the club. The phrase barely legal turned in its grave. "She's a child," he said quietly. Shame. His face burned.

"That's how you usually like them, isn't it? Trying to re-kindle some horse-shit with a Zoe-a-like."

Owen turned his head and stared deeply into the steering wheel.

"Gonna get you a boner tonight."

"Please," he breathed. "I don't ..."

"What? Want to? Yeah. Yeah you do. You wanted to with me, and you wanted to with countless before. You're a sack of shit lying paedophile, who can't get a hard-on, even for this," she gestured down at herself like she was on The Price Is Right, "let alone some hot poon like that."

Owen breathed in slowly.

"Well," she continued, "tonight, with my beautiful assistant," she jabbed her finger in the direction of the girl, "and me in the sack, you're finally getting some."

"I—" He turned to speak and she was gone. Dropped his head to the steering wheel. Stared into the foot well of the car. "Balls," he whispered. He knocked his head a couple of times on the leather and then raised his eyes to watch the girl, now walking into the club. He had a choice, right? Whatever was going on, he could just walk away. Leave her be. Return home.

To that thing.

That monster. Whatever she was. Whatever she claimed to be. He rested his hand down on the door handle. Looked down at himself, checking his suit. Owen got out the car, brushing himself down. Walked straight towards the door of the club. Look purposeful. Be in control.

―――

The girl's name was Sissy. She was sitting the passenger seat now. She'd had way more to drink than she could handle and being the gentleman he said he was, he'd offered to take her *home*. She was half-asleep before they'd gotten to the end of the road. Owen drove out the city.

It wasn't until they were parked outside his house that Sissy seemed to pay any attention to her surroundings.

She looked bleary eyed from the window. Into the darkness of the street. Squinting. Owen watched her. He noted that the Jenkin's daughter's bedroom light was still on. At this hour. Returning his gaze to her, he smiled. Warmly. Like a school teacher. They all seemed pre-disposed to respond to that warm, mature, authoritarian approach. She had smooth skin. Her make-up wasn't on right.

She'd said in the club she was sixteen. She ducked her head forward like it was a big secret, but she'd said it too loudly because she was drunk. Owen didn't mind. He'd found a place to sit at the bar where he didn't get a lot of attention, after all.

"We're here," he said.

Her confused face dropped into a frown. She wasn't expecting to be there. Clearly. "I don't live here," she said.

"Oh." Owen withdrew, his smile dropped, but not to anger. To practiced disappointment. "I'm sorry." He stammered slightly as he spoke. "I thought ..." His voice dropped away. He glanced to her. She was disarmed. He could see it in her face. "Silly old fool," he muttered. The girl's face dropped. She was feeling sorry for him. "Look," he said without looking at her. "Do you mind if I pop in. I just need the bathroom."

Sissy shook her head.

Owen pushed open the door. He glanced back at her. "Do you want to come in for a quick night-cap before I take you home." She hesitated. "To apologise?" He pulled his weakest, most pathetic smile.

Then she nodded.

Hook, line, and sinker. Worked like a charm. Every time.

Sissy opened the door of the car and got out. She waited patiently. Then followed Owen as he walked towards the house. The light to the side of the front door never came on. He'd switched it off in the house, just in case anyone ever saw him coming home late. So they couldn't see who he was with. Just because she said she was sixteen, didn't mean she was. And the neighbours would judge him.

His tastes.

Owen opened the front door. The inside of the house was dark. He let her in first before stepping in behind her and closing the front door, slipping the lights on at the same time. He half expected Emma to be there, laying across the sofa, but the room was empty, as he'd left it.

He excused himself, went to the kitchen, leaving Sissy to sit. He went and got a bottle of Aldi wine. She was never going to know the difference. He took the corkscrew out the cupboard and unfurled the wrapper from the top of the bottle. He looked at the screw top. Of course. He opened it, and left the cap behind. He wanted to ply her hard. Took two glasses from the cabinet.

Just as he picked the bottle up, he saw Emma. She was sitting on the counter. Hadn't been there before. "Got her?" she asked quietly.

Owen smiled. Nodded.

Emma clapped. Big, gleeful smile.

Owen frowned and shushed her.

"She can't hear me," she said. She slid down off the counter and looked around the door of the kitchen. "Not yet, anyway." She turned back to him. "So before we get this show on the road, are you going to tell me why you cut out women's reproductive organs?"

Owen almost dropped the wine. His stomach clenched. "What?" he asked quietly.

"I know, remember." She tapped the side of his temple. "I've been in here. I mean. *I* know why, but I want you to admit it. Before we get this party started." She smiled like butter wouldn't melt.

"I find the question distasteful," he said.

"Distasteful?" Emma nodded. "All right, then." Her smile grew. "After you." She stepped aside.

Owen left the kitchen. He tried to compose himself in the short walk to the sofa. Put on a face for the girl. Whatever her name was. He placed the glasses down, poured two. Large. White. She looked like the sort of girl who hadn't a taste for red.

Not yet.

Well, not ever. Not after tonight, anyway. Not the way things usually went.

She smiled. It seemed half-hearted. Took the glass and sipped. "So," she said. She seemed to have sobered up a little. But the wine should fix that.

CHAPTER 15

Owen was sitting in the armchair, his legs crossed. Sissy was sitting in the middle of the sofa. He was purposefully keeping his distance, remaining passive. Letting her guard get so far down, she wouldn't bring it back up. Third glass for her. He'd only had a few sips of the stuff. Her eyelids were getting a little heavier. He didn't want her unconscious, but having her worse for wear would help.

Pliable.

Emma was at the far end of the sofa, directly in Owen's line of sight, crouching, legs spread, on the cushion next to Sissy, only Sissy didn't have any idea that she was there. She could clearly neither hear her, nor see her.

Owen was beginning to wonder if he hadn't had a stroke when he was strangling Emma on the sofa last week and he was in a coma in hospital and all this was a dream.

Emma had her fingers in between her legs. Frigging herself. She was making grunts and groans like she hadn't cum in a month. "Fucking hell," she said. She was breathing hard. She'd been doing it for a few minutes, and putting Owen off his game entirely. "Get on with it," she breathed. She sounded *close.*

Owen shot her a glance when Sissy wasn't paying attention, as if to say, *shut up, I'm getting there.*

Emma cried out. Slowed a little. A whimper. "Tell her you're going to fuck her."

Owen looked away.

"Tell her."

"I want you," Owen said quietly. Sissy looked up at him. She seemed a little surprised, but he'd been pushed into the dad-zone before, and he'd still been able to make his move. She smiled a little.

"No," insisted Emma. "Use the exact words." She was huffing air in and out. "I'm going to fuck you."

Owen shook his head. Subtle enough that the girl wouldn't notice. That wasn't his style. He wasn't in-your-face. He wasn't the upfront *fuck you* type. Style. That's what it took to be him. When you looked like him. Were of an age.

Style.

Emma was still crouched, naked and spread legged, but she had at least stopped touching herself. "You're going to fuck me tonight, right? So you do it my way," she said. Haughty. She stood. Walked around the far side of the table to Owen's side.

He didn't move. Didn't acknowledge her. He was looking at Sissy. Returning her gaze. When Emma got up close to him, he could smell her sex.

She perched on the edge of the chair and reached down to his shirt. She pushed her hand gently into him. Through his clothes. Into his skin. Sliding through his bone.

Owen could feel her fingers next to his heart.

"Tell her," Emma whispered. "Tell her you're going to fuck her dead body." She squeezed his heart like it was a fresh fruit, testing it for ripeness. "Tell her now, or you're going to have a heart attack, right here in front of her. *Old man*."

"I … I …" he stammered for real this time. He could feel her fingers inside his body. They were cold on his organs. He could feel his blood splashing against her flesh. "I'm going to fuck you," he said. Hoped it was enough.

Sissy looked surprised. Eyes widened. She then glanced down to his crotch. It was involuntary, but Owen saw a sign that she was up for it.

He started to smile at her, when Emma's fingers tightened.

"The rest," she whispered.

Owen touched his head to his chest, feeling his heart start to lose rhythm. "I want to fuck your corpse," he blurted.

"Close enough," Emma said, releasing him. She stood quickly, retreating across the room.

Sissy dropped her wine glass, spilling the remains of the liquid everywhere. The glass shattered when it hit the edge of the coffee table.

Owen instinctively reached out, passively. He wanted to calm her, but it was too late. She was scared, and the night was over. But he couldn't let her leave.

He could hear Emma laughing in the corner. "Fucking hell," she was saying. "You really said it."

Owen pushed himself from the chair. He wasn't getting any younger. He grabbed out at the girl. She wasn't stable on her feet. Got his hand around her wrist. The two of them stood, for a split second, staring at each other, before she gave a quick yank to free herself. When that didn't work, she lunged back towards him. Hand balled into a fist. She punched him in the face. Clean on the nose. Owen heard a crack before he felt anything, and then the warmth of liquid gushing down his face. He still gripped her.

Couldn't let her leave. Not now. The police would come. There was evidence everywhere.

"You should be more afraid of your mortal soul." Emma was laughing as she spoke.

He reached forward, grabbed the little whore's hair and pulled her downwards. Towards the floor, overpowering her. She screamed. Loud. He heard something wet splashing. Now he'd gotten her head down, she'd thrown up over his feet. The smell rose. She screamed again.

Owen let her hair go. Kept hold of the other hand.

When she stood, Owen slapped her. Open palmed. As hard as he could. The sound of it burst out in the room. Bouncing off the walls. She stopped screaming. Reached up and touched her face. The wind taken from her for a split second. Then she looked by Owen. To the corner of the room. Her look changed from horror to surprise.

She looked at Emma.

Owen turned, looking between the two of them. "You can see her?" he said, no more than a whisper.

CHAPTER 16

Emma burst out laughing. "Yes," she screamed. Giggling. She was teasing her body with her fingers.

The neighbours. The commotion. *No.*

Sissy wailed. Started crying. Owen was still holding onto her. Everything was going wrong. He stared at Sissy. And it was all her fault. He clenched his fist. Anger rising within him like floodwaters about to pass over. Then Sissy lashed out. Suddenly. She punched him hard in the face again. Straight on the nose. Blood erupting from him like a burst water main. He reeled. Stumbled backwards.

He released her.

She screamed. Top of her voice. *Rape.*

Owen maintained his balance, stopping himself from going over the armchair. He glared quickly at Emma. She was laughing hard, and holding her crotch like she was going to piss. *Stop it*, she was saying. Waving her free hand at the two of them. *Fucking Laurel and Hardy.*

Jesus wept.

Owen turned his attention back to Sissy. The girl. She was making too much noise. He desperately flung himself forward, grabbing her on the shoulders, forcing her back. Onto the sofa. Dropping down on top of her. Using his weight to subdue her.

Sissy's eyes bounced between the two of them. "You fucking perverts," she hissed. "Fuck you." She started to wriggle.

Squirm.

Owen forced his bodyweight down onto her,

trying to stop her.

"It's okay," Emma said, coming up beside the two of them, having finally stopped laughing. "He won't dick you. Can't."

Owen scowled at her, and noted that she was making the pathetic-little-cock motion, dangling her little finger out.

"Can't get it hard, you see. Something to do with Zoe." She paused. "And the baby," Emma added at the end.

"No," Owen barked. He wanted to hit out at Emma. Shut her up. But he couldn't let go of the girl. She was going to escape.

"You fucking weirdo's," Sissy blurted. The tears had stopped now. Subsided to anger. Fear. Hate.

Owen felt her knee raise. Hard. The warmth turned to burning as pain blistered from his groin. She wriggled more. Then did it again. Sickness rose in his gut. Not enough to come out, but enough to stop him from paying quite as much attention to Sissy as he should have been. A slow darkness clouded his vision, just for a second, after the second knee landed. And then suddenly he was moving. Rolling. Away from the girl. Off the sofa.

He landed hard on the floor. The girl on top of him. Staring each other in the face. She head butted him. On his bloody nose. Pain smashed around in his frontal lobe, his brain rebooting. Owen grasped at his face, his burning face. Warm blood oozing out over his skin. Flares of white light in his vision.

He realised she was gone. Off him. The girl. She was getting away. She'd call the police. He squinted his eyes open as best he could. But she was stood over him. She spat on him. She had blood on her face, but it was his, he suspected. He let his hands drop, shaking, from his face. Looked at them, bloody too. His nose had gone numb. Feeling gone. Head rocking a splitting headache. The motherfucker of all headaches.

The two of them were stood over him, together.

"He's a dirty cunt," said Emma. "Holding me here. Captive." She put her arm around the young girl. "We should call the police," she said.

It was over. Owen rested his head back. His fight was gone. Nothing left but the want to lay on the floor and bleed.

"Or we can make him pay," said Sissy.

Owen pulled his eyes open a little.

What?

CHAPTER 17

Emma laughed a little. She squeezed Sissy tightly. "If you want," she said. "It's your call."

Owen tried to push himself up on his elbows, and Emma stopped him. Bare foot into his chest. He looked up her naked body. Her skin glistened under the glow of the light. She pushed him back to the floor. "Pathetic," she said.

"I want," Sissy whispered. She pushed her hand into her jacket pocket and pulled something out.

Owen couldn't see what.

She leaned down. Pushed something towards him. Into his face and then his vision was filled with mist. Burning in his nose. His mouth. His eyes started to water. His skin itched. It was on fire. Owen shook his head from side to side. Trying to make it stop. Covered his face. He screamed out.

Pepper spray.

He could taste it.

Then Emma dropped down onto him. She landed hard on his chest. Knees first. "Gonna fuck," she whispered. It wasn't loud enough for Sissy to hear. Not over the giggling she was making, mumbling about him looking like a burnt cherry now. Emma slapped him. "Tell me." She said. "Tell me who Zoe was?"

Owen's tears streamed down his face. He told himself it was from the pepper spray. Not the humiliation of these two fucking with him. "I can't, she died," he cried. "My child took her." He looked away, embarrassed.

"And that stopped your pathetic cock from working?" Emma was screaming into his face. Bellowing. Angry. "Giving you the right to fucking murder people?" She spat on him. Just as Sissy had. Gobbed wet, slimy, sputum into his face. Mixing with his sticky, gelatinous blood, still weeping from his nose. She punched him. A wet splat as the blood and mucus sprayed from his face.

Owen's head banged hard on the floor beneath. Blood let from his mouth. Bitten his tongue. Broken his teeth. She hit like a bulldozer. Otherworldly.

"Please," he whispered.

"Thought some power over women might make it work again?" She looked up at Sissy. "Picking on the young one's that can't protect themselves?"

"Fucker," Sissy said. She stepped around the side of the two of them and pushed her foot into Owen's broken and bleeding nose, splitting it further.

"I've seen inside you," Emma hissed. "I know what you'd never admit." She reached around. Behind her. Loosened his belt. Slid her hand inside. Touched his flaccid cock. "I know what makes you … tick."

Owen's cock twitched.

"And there it is," she said. She moved her hand away from him. Back to his face. Visible after Sissy had moved her foot.

Owen lay there. Confused. Harder than he had been in thirty or more years. Since the death of Zoe his first love. Giving birth to the child that killed her. Leaving him alone. Unloveble. Dead on the inside. Full of hatred on the out.

Owen closed his eyes, darkness taking his

consciousness.

CHAPTER 18

Pain. Pain that at first felt as if it were everywhere, was only in his face. It shrouded his head. Made it feel worse than it was. Owen opened his eyes. Looked quickly around the room. He was in the bedroom. He was on the bed.

Bound.

Spread-eagle like the whores he tortured.

There was Emma. She was sitting in the chair that he usually sat in. She was reading his book. Shaking her head. Tut. Snort. It wasn't a comedy, yet she seemed to be finding great humour in it. She flipped the page.

Owen tried to speak. Couldn't move his mouth properly. Words came out as a grunt. A muffled shriek. He couldn't close his mouth. The ball-gag. She'd strapped him up like he was one of *them*. She was looking at him, as he tried to see the gag in his mouth. It didn't matter which way he turned his head. He couldn't see it.

Emma put the book down and crossed her legs. Naked. She was always naked. She stood up, walked over to him without speaking. And all Owen could do was stare at her, wide-eyed. Afraid. She ran her fingernails up his torso. The feeling of a sensual touch enraged his cock immediately. Hard. So hard it hurt. Like the last thirty years of subservience had been lifted and he was free. Free at last. "That's it," she said. "You're all better now." She spoke quietly. A husk in her voice. Like she was enjoying having him there. Bound and gagged. Free to do whatever she wished to him.

The thought made him harder.

"You just needed to let a woman," she tilted her head, "or two, take control. So filled with hate and anger, that you couldn't see the wood for the trees. Or the bush, come to that." She grinned, turned away. Giggled. "Wood," she said, quietly. Owen looked wildly around the room. The other girl. Whatever her name was. She wasn't there.

His eyes were drawn to Emma. She was at his chest of drawers. Pulled open the second one. *She had been inside his mind.* She pulled out his blade. The one he'd used on the girls. The one he used when he wasn't satisfied.

It looked bigger, now he was tied to the bed and watching.

Jesus.

She needled the tip of it into her finger, withdrawing her flesh, made a hiss like it hurt. Then she rubbed her fingers together. Wiping away the prick. Her eyes drifted from the knife to him. Smiled. A thin smile. Told a tale.

Owen looked down at his hard cock. Laying there. Waiting. Nothing to do, but wait. She came over to him. Ran the flat of the cold blade down his skin. Raising the hairs on his chest. Goose bumps up.

"You seem to like it," she said. "You seem to like the idea of being dominated." Her voice was smooth. Soft. Quiet. A whisper. She scraped the tip of the blade over his nipple. It was sharp. Dug in. Drew the smallest pin-prick of blood.

Owen stopped breathing. Held the air in his body, waiting to see what she was going to do next. She'd promised to fuck him. Make him fuck her. She had *promised*.

"Close your eyes," she said. "I have a surprise."

Owen stared at her. Not with the knife in her hand. He was not going to look away.

She placed her hand on his forehead and slid it down over his face like he was already a corpse, staring into the abyss. He did it. His mind said no, but his body let his eyes shut. He smiled. The thoughts of what this surprise was going to be, rampant in his mind. He couldn't wait. Opened them within seconds.

She was on the other side of the room. Facing the chair. The wall. She'd put her weight on one hip over the other. Very sexy. She was still holding the knife. He couldn't see it, but he could tell she was holding something. She turned.

She'd changed. She looked different.

At first, Owen noticed that her skin had changed to a lighter, mottled, pale. His eyes drifted over her nakedness. Her tits hung down a little lower than before. Her belly sagged. The flesh torn open. A chasm, gaped. There was a hole where her guts should have been. Gone. Missing. Dried, black, clots of blood clung to her. The tattoos that adorned her skin had lost vibrancy. He looked wildly at her hair. Dried. Poking out at all angles.

She was nodding as he took her in. "Yes," she said. "This is what I look like now. At the bottom of that hole you left me in." She wagged the knife at him. "Not so healthy looking now, am I right?"

Owen didn't know what to make of it at first. She looked different. But his cock was still hard. He still wanted her. Something was wrong in his mind. He couldn't want to fuck … that. It was still her, he supposed, the thoughts crashing around, confused. Just *deader*. Then the smell hit him. The stink of something rotting. A week in a quarry. Decomposing flesh. She stepped over to him. The smell got stronger. His stomach turned. Couldn't stop it. Vomit rushed his gullet and fought around the ball-gag, choking him. He thrashed his head, unable to breath. Coughing the vomit up, trying to get it passed his teeth. The burning of the bile on his tongue. He could feel it *in his nose*. Swallowed the gelatinous puke back. Allowing his airways freedom.

She started laughing. "They'll be here soon," she said, pointing the knife at the window.

Owen coughed, tried to say, *who*, but nothing came out. It just made him cough more.

"The police," she said, as if she was still reading his mind. "Little Sissy has gone to get them."

Owen nodded. The game was up.

CHAPTER 19

"Be a shame though, if you went to jail for hitting on some skanky teen and beating her up a little ... wouldn't it?" She looked down at his cock. Sat down on the bed next to him.

Owen writhed, trying to get away from her. His burning erection lied about how he was feeling. Now he had it, the dirty fucking thing wouldn't go away.

Emma slipped her rotting, cold, fleshy hand around his shaft and held him. The feeling was as much serene ecstasy as vile revulsion. The touch so good. The flesh so bad. He thought she was going to pleasure him, but she just held him, for a second. He turned his head away. Tried to ignore the smell of her. Tried to stop *tasting* it. Then he felt the sharp pain. Like she was gripping him too hard.

He turned his head back. Looked at her. She was studying him. His member. Intently, like she was trying to do something intensely complicated. His cock was burning. He raised his head up and looked at it.

Her hand gripping its length. The other, working the knife around the root of it. Where the shaft met the skin. The steel of the blade sliding into his flesh.

Owen screamed out as the pain ruptured up his torso. He tried to move away from her, but all he managed to do was squirm. She snapped her head to look at him. A frown. "You'll make this a whole lot worse if you struggle," she said. Her ice, vice, grip stopping him anyway.

The burning was too much, and Owen started

banging his head up and down on the pillow behind it. Yelling. Trying to beg her to stop.

But he never lost his erection.

She slid the blade under the base of his skin. Through to the corpus below, but not cutting through that. Twisting the blade around the circumference of his cock, until the skin was nothing more than a glove. Then she dragged it up the length of his shaft, de-gloving his penis of its skin.

Holding it like a bloody, used condom over his body.

Owen screamed as the pain of it stabbed at him like a thousand knives. Blood slopped down from the skin-dom she was holding, dribbling blood like cum onto his torso. He thrashed, feeling like a field of stinging nettles was being dragged over his whole body, the skin being grated off, lemon juice and vinegar poured over every inch. He looked down to his cock. It looked like a hot dog, drenched in hot sauce.

Felt like it too.

Emma laughed. She touched it to her lips.

Owen's skinless cock dribbled blood down into his pubes turning them into a sticky matted mess. He was weeping. The dried blood in his nose from earlier wetted by the puke that had gotten up there. He'd chipped several of his teeth on the cheap ball gag. Could feel them. Cutting into his tongue. The inside of his mouth.

Emma stood. She took the knife and the skin. Over to the chair. Sat. Naked. Spread legs, offering Owen the view of her cunt. "They'll be here soon. Think they'll find you, or are you going to bleed out?

Can you even bleed out from that wound?" She raised his cock skin to her face and looked at it. "I wonder if they could even sew it back on?"

Owen couldn't focus. He thought he must have been losing blood, but in actuality it was shock.

"Better be sure," she said. Emma slipped Owen's cock-dom skin sheath over the blade of the knife.

She sat back in the chair and raised each of her legs over the arms. Spread her legs so far that she nearly split in two.

"After all …" She smiled. Broad. "I'm already dead."

CHAPTER 20

Emma took the knife wearing Owen's cock sheath, and turned it to face her. His prick-head facing her opening.

Owen couldn't take his eyes from the scene. The bizarre macabre-ness holding what was left of his consciousness. Black clouding his vision.

Emma looked at him. "Fuck me, lover," she said. She drew the blade towards her, stabbing the sharp steel into her cunt, mashing and slicing the cock sheath, the two of them bleeding together. Becoming one. She stuffed the blade into her hard, up to the hilt. Then pulled it out. Black, clotted blood sprayed from her gash, torn and slashed to a macabre new opening. The mother cunt. "Fuck me harder," she screamed, pushing the blade in, pulling it out. Over and over. The knife cutting chunks of the woman away as her long dead blood flowed out, onto the fabric of the armchair. Dripping and sliding down, onto the carpet beneath. Pieces of her meat pulled along by the river of black plasma. Dead, rotting, blood.

She fucked the knife. Again and again. Her crotch becoming an unidentifiable bloody mess. "Yes," she started saying, getting louder. She screamed as she feigned orgasm. Once. Twice. Her inners pushing out through the chasm she created with the blade. Her bladder, sex organs, all becoming one slick, sticky, black mess of meat and offal.

Owen watched, until he could watch no more. He rested his head down on the pillow. Light headed. Blood not where it should have been. Parts of him cut off.

"He will be pleased," she squealed, the knife fucking into her so far now it had reached her guts, splitting her corpse open further until what was left of her inners gushed out, slopping down to the floor. The smell of the dead razing all else in the room.

And Owen closed his eyes.

Praying for death to take him.

———

Owen regained consciousness to the sound of a man say, "Jesus fucking Christ." More than once. He was saying it over and over. He pulled his eyes open. Laying on the bed. There were people.

Lots and lots of people.

He could see men in suits. Men in uniform. Paramedics.

He moved his hands. They were down by his side as if they had never been tied up. He moved his jaw, free of the ball gag.

"He's awake," said one of the medics.

The man blaspheming about Christ stopped doing it, and drew his head over Owen. Looked him in the eyes. "Man, you are some sicko fuck." His colleague slapped his arm with the back of his hand. "What? He'd not going to remember any of this, is he?"

Owen glanced down his body. His cock was all back together. Sheathed. A dream. A vision? Who knew? Who cared? He was whole again. In trouble for touching that little bitch ... whatever her name was.

"You don't think you're getting away with it that easily, do you?"

Owen turned his head. Emma was laying naked on the bed next to him. She was stroking the tattoo on her chest. The fat little devil. *Kinky cultist*. He smiled at her.

"What's he looking at?"

Owen looked back up to the police officer. A glance to the bed next to him, and she was gone. Maybe it was all in his head. Only the girl would be able to say … if she'd seen Emma or not.

"Why's this sicko smiling?"

A uniform copper handed him a bag of white powder. "Found this in the drawer downstairs, Guv." The man looked at it. Nodded. Returned his look to Owen.

Owen could hear something strange. Sounded like the morning after a heavy night.

Someone clear that up.

He raised his head and looked over towards the door. There was a copper in uniform. Had his head down. Vomit streaming from his mouth. Wiping it with his uniformed arm. Owen frowned. Gazed around the room.

Emma was there. On the chair. She was gutted. Blood everywhere.

Then Owen realised that the room still smelt of the pungency of her rotting flesh. Her week old innards. Spilt to the floor. His knife in the clotted black mess on the carpet. He looked down at himself, naked on the bed, where they had found him.

Hard.

About the Author

Ash is a British horror author. He resides in the south, in the Garden of England. He writes horror that is sometimes fantastical, sometimes grounded, but always deeply graphic, and black with humour.

Made in the USA
Columbia, SC
13 June 2024